Holly Prickles The Hedgehog

Book One

Holly Prickles Finds a New Home

Happy Reading

Brenda May Williams

This book is purely fictional.

Illustrated by Raymond Williams

Cover by R.C. Bean

Edited by Alec Hawkes

Publishing assistance by Elizabeth Mills

Written with love for May and Ann

Hello Boys and Girls.

How would you like to hear a story about Holly Prickles the hedgehog? In this story she finds a lovely new house for herself and all of her friends.

Gather round and I will begin.

Holly Prickles, a sweet and unusual Hedgehog indeed, lives in a beautiful garden at Number 5 Cheery Lane in the village of Puddlesplash.

She is a very popular hedgehog and has lots of friends.

Holly is unusual because everyone knows that hedgehogs live alone but not Holly. Holly lives with her friends so you can see how this would make her different from all of the other hedgehogs can't you?

Holly Prickles finds a new home.

One day Holly woke up under the hedgerow that she shared with her friends. It had rained the night before and there was a beautiful rainbow across the sky. When Holly woke up she was cold and wet, all of the leaves that she had gathered for her bed were soggy.

Holly was miserable, she had a runny nose and she just could not stop sneezing. She had caught a terrible cold and all she wanted to do was go outside to gather her breakfast and go back to sleep. Holly knew that she had to go and find breakfast herself, she was a big hedgehog now and that's what big hedgehogs do.

Holly wobbled out from under her hedgerow to see what she could find, she scrambled around in the undergrowth and found her favourite thing to eat, a big, ripe strawberry.

She could not believe her luck, she tucked into the juicy strawberry and when her tummy was full she was happy. But, Holly had a runny nose and she was still sneezing.

Holly Prickles decided that she really must go back to bed and have a rest, then maybe she would feel better.

She wobbled back under her hedgerow and was very
annoyed to find her best friend Squiggles the Worm was in
her pile of leaves.

Now the leaves were even more cold and damp. Holly knew that she would need to find some dry ones later, but this was her bed and it had taken her a long time to make it.

"What are you doing in my bed? You squiggly worm, don't you know that it is rude to take another creature's bed?" She shouted loudly at Squiggles.

Squiggles was just settling down for a nap and the loud shout had startled him.

Wriggling out from under a soggy leaf, he looked up in surprise.

"Oh, I am sorry Holly but I thought that you had finished with it for the day, it is all wet. Let me help you find some dry leaves for another bed and we can share it together." He said.

Holly smiled, she realised that she had shouted at Squiggles and she had been very, very loud. She felt sorry and kindly thanked him for his offer to help her find some dry leaves.

Feeling excited, she turned to Squiggles and smiled.

"Let's go and see what we can find".

They wandered in and out of the hedgerow collecting some twigs and leaves. When they were finished they had a lovely pile of dry bedding.

Holly knew that poor Squiggles had been helping her for a long time and he had not had time to look for anything to eat.

"Come on Squiggles, let us go and look for your breakfast, you must be hungry."

Squiggles nodded. The two friends set off and before long they stumbled across his favourite thing to eat. A big, juicy, green dandelion leaf.

Squiggles tucked in and when his tummy was full he was very happy indeed.

"That was the nicest dandelion leaf that I have ever tasted, but now I am very tired. Shall we go and have a rest in our warm dry bed?"

Squiggles smiled, rubbing his tummy.

Holly thought that this was a wonderful idea because she still had a runny nose and now her feet were sore.

And so the two friends wobbled and wriggled their way back to their hedgerow to rest in their lovely new bed.

But, when they arrived at the hedgerow they were very angry to find that George the Beetle had already settled down on top of their dry bed of leaves.

"What are you doing on our pile of leaves, you crawly beetle? It took ages for us to find those dry leaves. Go away and find your own bed."

Poor George was upset.

"I thought that it looked very comfortable and I have had the most awful night Holly, my wings are wet and my nose is running. I am sorry. I will go away and let you have your lovely, warm, bed back."

George looked at the floor and his face became very sad.

Holly and Squiggles felt sorry for poor George.

Squiggles asked him if he had eaten any breakfast. But poor George was still upset, he snivelled and wiped his nose. He told them that he had been too tired to look for his breakfast because the rain had washed him out of his home and now it was flooded.

Squiggles felt sorry for him.

"I am sorry that you were washed out of your home George. Would you like us to help you look for your breakfast?"

George cheered up. "Oh, yes please. You two are the best friends a beetle could have. I am very lucky to have such wonderful friends. Now where shall we look?" He said, feeling happier.

Holly pointed to the compost heap.

"Look over there George, I think that we may find a carrot in that pile. Shall we go and find out?" Holly smiled.

So Holly, Squiggles and George set off across the garden in search of George's breakfast.

To his delight, Squiggles found a lovely ripe carrot and he gave it to George.

A Carrot.

George's eyes lit up and he happily began to munch on the carrot. He was very hungry and when his tummy was full he let out a very big yawn.

"Carrots are my favourite thing in all the world. I love them. I thought that I would never find my breakfast today. But, thanks to my friends, I have a full tummy. Thank you for helping me." George said.

All three friends were very tired after finding a new dry bed and their breakfast. Holly and George still had runny noses. The thought of the lovely warm pile of leaves waiting for them under the hedgerow was just too much to resist. So, they made their way back across the garden to settle down for a nap.

To their horror, they noticed that the leaves were being carried away by Mr. Adams and his family of ants.

Holly, Squiggles and George were not going to let anyone steal their bed.

They gave chase and caught up with Mr. Adams and the ants just before they disappeared over the hill.

"Where are you going with our leaves, you sneaky little ants? We have spent all morning collecting those and we were just about to settle down for a nap."

"We need these leaves. We have a long way to travel back to our home. We need them to keep us dry. You will just have to find some more." Mr. Adams called back.

Holly was furious. She decided that it was up to her to find a home for everyone in the garden. After all, if they were going to share things, there really had to be order. "There are other leaves that you can have. I've seen them." Said Holly.

"I have seen the pile of dry leaves that Holly means," said one of the other ants, "I must say that they are just what we need for our home. We are the only ants in this garden, so we can take them all." Mr. Adams loved his family and he wanted to make sure that they were dry.

Only dry leaves would do.

An Oak Leaf

    "Quick march Holly Prickles, you take the lead," Mr. Adams ordered.

    Holly told Mr. Adams that she would be delighted to lead the way to find the best leaves. But first she insisted that the ants stack the leaves that they had stolen into a neat pile back under their hedgerow.

Everyone knows that ants work as a team and when Mr. Adams gave the order to stack the leaves in a neat pile, every ant fell into line. They put them back where they had found them and when they were finished, the bed looked better than it had before.

All three friends were very happy indeed.

"Come on Squiggles, come on George, let's help these ants find the best leaves for their home." Holly said. "I know just where they are."

They set out across the garden to the oak tree. It was just shedding its leaves. Holly told Mr. Adams that the best ones were at the bottom of the pile because the ones on the top were damp.

The ants were delighted.

"Thank you Holly Prickles, if you ever consider joining our colony you only have to mention my name." Said Mr. Adams.

Giving the order for his ants to collect as many leaves as possible, he marched them back up the hill and all the way home.

This really had been a very busy morning for everyone. It was almost lunchtime and they were all very tired.

Off they headed, back to the hedgerow, to settle down in their warm bed for a little nap before lunch.

All of a sudden Holly noticed that Ruby the Robin was
eyeing up their pile of leaves.

"Ruby, don't you dare take any of those leaves, fly away
up to the oak tree and keep your beak out of our bed."
Called Holly.

A Robin

Ruby was annoyed.

"Do you call that a bed? Those ants have taken all of the best leaves. I know where there is a little house that you can have, it would make a much more suitable home."

George was very interested in this little house. He was tired of being swept out of his home every time it rained because he always caught a cold.

Holly was very interested in this little house too. She was tired of being wet when it had rained, she always caught a cold.

Squiggles was very interested in this little house as well. He was tired of getting into trouble for making Holly's bed wet because he was a squiggly worm.

George asked Ruby where the house was. Ruby hopped along the grass and told them all about it. She said that a little girl who lived in the big house had outgrown some of her toys.

They had put her pink dolls house in the shed.

"I am very good friends with Ginger the Fox. If I ask him nicely he will push the dolls house onto the lawn and you can all live there." Ruby said.

Holly felt horrid about being so rude to Ruby. She held her head in shame.

Snuggling up against Ruby, being very careful not to prickle her with her spines, she smiled.

"Oh Ruby, you are the best friend that we could ever have. Do you really think that Ginger will help us to get the dolls house onto the lawn?"

"We will have a beautiful dry house in no time," said Ruby, and then flew away. In a flash she returned with Ginger the Fox. Ginger was not the smartest fox in the world but he was very strong. He said that he would help, so off he went into the shed.

He came back out pushing the dolls house along the grass with his big, strong snout.

"Okay Holly Prickles," he shouted, "You are the leader, where do you want me to put your new house?"

Everyone decided that it should be under the oak tree. There they could all be together and see each other every day.

Ginger pushed it up the hill, past the compost heap, and placed it right under the beautiful oak tree next to the dandelion patch.

A Dandelion

Squiggles was delighted because now he did not need to travel very far to find his favourite food. Squiggles thanked Ginger.

Holly was also delighted with the house because she would now have a warm dry bed.

"Look Holly," said Squiggles, excitedly. "The strawberries are close by too. We will all have full tummies."

Poor George had a long way to go to reach the compost heap, but he was not going to complain because he knew that his friends would help him to find ripe carrots every day.

Best of all, he also knew that he was never going to be washed out of his home during a rain storm ever again.

Holly Prickles had found a new home

Everyone was thrilled with their new house and busily set about making it their home. That night Holly, Squiggles and George could hear the rain hitting the roof of the old dolls house, their new home. They all smiled, knowing they were warm and dry. They all fell asleep and had lovely dreams.

The next morning when they woke up they all felt wonderful and there was another beautiful rainbow arched across the sky.

A Rainbow

Holly's feet no longer ached and her nose had stopped running. Squiggles stretched his long body and said that he felt wonderful.

As for George, well he had been up for hours and was already happily eating a carrot. George was very pleased that his wings were dry for a change, so he wanted to thank his friends for letting him share the house.

The happy beetle had been busily collecting everyone's breakfast. He had found a strawberry for Holly and a big pile of dandelion leaves for Squiggles. He left them on the pink doorstep of the new house.

Holly and Squiggles found their treats and they both jumped for joy. But best of all they made friends with all the other creatures who shared their garden.

Perry-Winkle the Mouse popped in for a visit.

He marvelled at the lovely pink house. "Good morning my friends, welcome to this lovely part of the garden."

Holly knew that they would be very happy living here. It really was the most beautiful new house that anyone could ever wish for and the most beautiful garden too!

Holly Prickles and her friends happily tucked into breakfast in the sunshine.

A Strawberry, a Carrot and a Dandelion

Who eats these for breakfast? Can you write their names?

Summary Page

I hope that you all enjoyed my little book about Holly and her friends.

As you can see, boys and girls, they are all very happy indeed living in their beautiful new house in the garden.

They hope that you will be able to drop by one day and pay them a visit but, until then …

Goodnight, sleep tight.

Love from

Brenda May.

Can you draw Holly here?

Can you draw George here?

Can you draw Squiggles here?

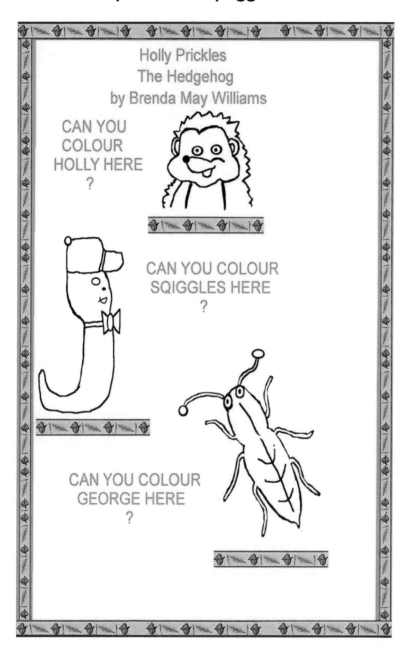

Also by Brenda May:

The Unusual Pet Shop

The Unusual Pet Shop is a place where pets wait to get their new forever homes. Parker the Nosy Parrot is so nosy that nobody wants him around. But he is also helpful, and tries to help everyone who he meets.

Mandu the Cat loves mice. A farmer takes Mandu home to get rid of the mice in his barn, but instead, Mandu makes friends with the mice and the farmer is annoyed.

Bob the Big Green Fish enjoys eating peas and "goes green." But a little girl takes him home and feeds him carrots, so Bob the Big Green Fish turns gold as he swims happily away.

Says the author: "Hello children! I hope you enjoy this lovely little book about these unusual pets, because it will not be long before you can read my next book about other pets that live in The Unusual Pet Shop."

Love from Brenda May.

Brenda May Williams plans to write four books in her series of unusual pets. She is inspired by her own pets that do all kinds of funny things.

The Shop of Magical Things

The Shop of Magical Things is a lovely little book all about a mystery shop that is looked after by Pat and her pet mice, and some of the occupants who live there. That is not the magical part of the shop, though - a fairy named Clare lives in the Shop of Magical Things and when it closes, she sprinkles magic glitter on the occupants and they come to life.

You will meet characters such as Pip, who is sad when he arrives at the shop but when Clare sprinkles him with her glitter he instantly cheers up and starts to sing and dance.

Mollie the Bear is very brave and loves the smell of honey, but she has never tasted it because she is a toy bear. When she is sprinkled with the glitter, she can also taste the lovely treat.

Amy the Dustpan Dolly is old and broken, Pat gives her some new straw and she is as good as new. When Clare sprinkles her with the glitter she instantly becomes busy and rushes around the shop collecting all of the crumbs on the way.

And the star attraction is Tommy, the pencil who draws beautiful rainbows on every book in the shop.

Pat and the mice are amazed by all of the magic that happens at the shop and you will be too.

The House of Useful Things

A lovely little book all about Mr and Mrs Green and their daughter Penny.

Mr and Mrs Green are avid recyclers and they never throw anything away if they think it has another purpose. Mack The Old Coat, is very old but one day Mrs Green decides to use him as a dress-up outfit for Penny and from then on Mack becomes the star attraction for Penny and her friends to wear to parties, Mack is happy because he is useful.

Stuffy Wuffy The Old Pillow, has lost some of his stuffing and Mrs Green stores him in the garage. He is very sad until one day he is taken out and used to make a lovely resting place for the new family pet, he is very happy to be so useful.

Kellie The Old Wellie has lost her partner, but Mr Green finds a great new use for Kelly, he decorates her with bright paint and she becomes a very unusual plant container, she loves her new look and makes friends with all the occupants of the garden.

Jock The Old Sock is on the washing line one day when his partner, Rock, is blown away. He is very sad but he is used for a variety of useful things and he happily waits until the day Rock is found and they are a pair again.

Coming Soon;

Marvin and the Magical Melody Mice

Made in the USA
Charleston, SC
18 September 2014